THE MAGIC PAPER

Tana Reiff

GLOBE FEARON
Pacemaker Curriculum Group

HOPES *And* DREAMS

Cover Photo: AP/Wide World Photos
Illustration: Tennessee Dixon

ISBN 0-8224-3686-8
Printed in the United States of America

9 10 11 12 13   07 06 05 04

Globe
Fearon

Pearson Learning Group

1-800-321-3106
www.pearsonlearning.com

CONTENTS

CHAPTER 1

Mexico City, Mexico,
1980

The line
of people
looked a mile long.
It seemed as if
half of Mexico
wanted a visa today.
The line moved
very slowly.

Lupe Garcia
had been here
since early morning.
Now it was 3:00.
She was hungry.
Sometimes she sat
on the ground
to rest her feet.

Then she felt
a little push.
She turned around.
"You need a visa?"
a young man asked her.

"Yes,"
said Lupe.
"I only want
to visit my aunt and uncle.
They live in Los Angeles.
I don't even want
to stay in the U.S.
My family is here
in Mexico City."

"You will never
get a visa here,"
the young man whispered.
"Many people
are turned down.
I can get you
a visa fast."

"A real visa?"
Lupe asked.

"It will look real.
That is all that matters,"
said the man.
"You give me
your *pesos*.
I'll bring your visa
in one hour."

Lupe walked away
from the long line.

The young man
led her
around the corner.
He took her picture.
Then he took her money.

"I'll be back
in one hour,"
he said.
"You have my word."

Lupe waited.
She wondered
if she had done
the right thing.

What if the fake visa
was not OK?
Or what if the man
ran away
with her money?

But an hour later,
the young man
was back.
He handed Lupe
her new visa.
"Have a good trip,"
he smiled.

The next day
Lupe said goodbye
to her family.
She walked
to the bus station.
She got on a bus
going north.
That night
the bus
pulled into Los Angeles.

Thinking It Over

1. If you were Lupe
   would you have given money
   to a stranger?

2. Why do you think
   Lupe agreed to buy
   a fake visa?

3. Do you believe
   everything people tell you?

CHAPTER **2**

"Los Angeles
is so nice!"
said Lupe.
"It makes me see
how very poor
Mexico is!
Here there are jobs.
People can eat
whenever they are hungry.

"This is true,"
said Aunt Juana.
"We have never
run out of food.
We are far from rich.
But we are not
dirt poor either."

"Do you think
I could work
while I am here?"

asked Lupe.
"I would love
to send money home.
My family
could really use it.
If I send enough,
my sister Raquel
would come north, too."

"You are not
supposed to work,"
said Aunt Juana.
"You do not have
the right kind of visa."

"I can find you work,"
said Uncle Ruben.
"You can work
in a dress factory.
No one there
will check your visa."

So Lupe
went to work
in the dress factory.
She did not get paid

by the hour.
She did piece work.
She got paid
for only the work
she finished.
The faster she worked,
the more money
she made.
She worked
12 hours a day
to make more money.

One day
Lupe's nose
began to run.
It must be a cold,
she said to herself.
But days later,
her nose still ran.
She felt hot
all the time.
Soon she got so sick,
she could not go
to work.
She got
no sick pay.

"You are not well,
my dear,"
said Aunt Juana.
"I will
take care of you.
I think
the dress factory
made you sick.
The air
in that place
can get pretty thick."

"There is something
I must tell you,"
Lupe began.
"I have already stayed
in the U.S.
too long.
My visa
is no good now.
This would be
a good time
to go back to Mexico."

"You cannot go
when you are so sick,"

said Aunt Juana.
"You must stay here
until you feel better."

But when Lupe got better,
she did not want
to leave.
There were no jobs
back home.
She could never make money
like she did
in the factory.
Her family
was better off
if she worked here.

"Stay with us
as long as you wish,"
said Uncle Ruben.
"Your aunt and I
have green cards.
We may live here
as long as we want.
But lots of people
live here
without papers."

"I don't want Lupe
to get into trouble,"
said Aunt Juana.

"What do you think
is the worst thing
that could happen?"
asked Uncle Ruben.
"They would tell her
to go home.
Then she could leave."

"I will stay
for a few months,"
said Lupe.
"I will find
a new job.
But I'm afraid
I will not feel safe.
I will look
around every corner.
I will always be afraid
of getting caught."

Thinking It Over

1. Do you think
   Lupe is doing
   the right thing
   to stay in the U.S.?

2. Why was Lupe
   willing to work
   12 hours a day?

CHAPTER 3

Back in Mexico
there was a young man
named Benito Cruz.
He lived
in a small town
out in the country.
The town
was very poor.
There were not enough jobs
for all the people.
Young men and old men
sat along the street.
They sat and talked
all day long.
There was nothing else
to do.

Benito sat
with the other men.
"I have gone north
and back again

five or six times,"
he told them.
"I have gone
by bus,
by train,
by car,
by river.
I always came back
because this is home.
But no one here
will give me a job.
They say
I had it too good
up north.
Here, a day's pay
is the same as
an hour's pay
in California."

"What will you do?"
said one old man.

"Head north again,"
said Benito.
"I can always get
farm work up there."

"One of these days
you will get caught
at the border,"
said the old man.

"It is better
to get caught there
than not eat here,"
laughed Benito.

The next day
Benito walked
to the main road.
He looked
for a ride.
A truck stopped.

"I'll take you
as far as the border,"
said the driver.
"You must cross
on your own."

But they got
only a few miles
down the road.

A policeman
stopped the truck.

"Don't lie to me,"
said the policeman.
"I know
where you are going.
How badly
do you want
to get there?"

"Very badly,"
said Benito.

"I'll let you pass,"
said the policeman.
"But first you pay me
150 dollars.
It's just a small fine."

Benito handed over
150 American dollars.
The truck rolled on.

At Tijuana,
Benito waited for help

to cross the border.
He walked around
until he found
a *coyote*.

"I need a bus ride
into California,"
Benito told the man.

"Give me 200 dollars,"
said the coyote.

Benito gave him
the money.
Now Benito
had used up
almost all of his money.

"No bus rides today,"
said the coyote.
"The border
is too hot today."

He led Benito
to a big pipe
that ran under the ground.

"This is your way
into the U.S.,"
said the coyote.
"Just climb inside
and keep going
to the end."

Benito
did not move.

"Hurry up,"
said the man.
"If we stand here
too long,
we will be caught."

Benito
did as he was told.
He got down
on his hands and knees.
He climbed into the pipe.
It was dark and wet.
The air smelled bad.
Benito pulled himself
inch by inch.
He must have gone a mile.

It seemed like hours
had gone by.
It was hard to breathe.
Benito tried
to raise his head.
He bumped against
the top of the pipe.
Benito got scared.
What if he
couldn't make it
to the other end?
He felt something
crawl over his legs.
Could that be a rat?
Benito moved faster.

At last,
there was light
ahead of him.
Finally, Benito
climbed out of the pipe.
He lay on the ground.
The fresh air
felt good.
Benito was in the U.S.!
He was safe!

Thinking It Over

1. Would you go
   to the trouble Benito did
   to cross into the U.S.?

2. What do you think
   of the policeman
   who took Benito's money?

3. What other escape stories
   have you ever heard?

CHAPTER **4**

Benito Cruz
went to work
in the fields.
He moved
from farm to farm.
He picked
whatever vegetables
were in season.

Many of the other workers
had families.
Benito spent
most of his off hours
with the young single men.
Now and then
they went
to Los Angeles
to have a good time.

Still,
Benito wanted

his own family.
He knew
he could not get married here.
To get married,
a person
must be legal.
Benito wished
he were legal.

One night in town,
Benito was having a drink.
He started talking
to a stranger.
"I can get you
an American wife,"
said the man.
"If you marry
an American,
you can get
a green card.
Then you can live
in the U.S.
as long as you want.
You can get married
and become legal
all at once!"

It sounded
like a good idea
to Benito.
"How much
must I pay you?"
he asked.

"Just 800 dollars!"
said the man.
"I would like
to do it for nothing.
I like
to make people happy.
But I have costs—
know what I mean?"

"For just 800 dollars
I can be
legal *and* married?"
asked Benito.

"Sure,"
said the man.
"Add a few dollars
for the lawyer,
of course."

"This sounds
good to me,"
said Benito.

"I will bring the woman
to this place,"
said the man.
"Be here
next Friday night
at 8:00."

Benito came back
the next Friday.
He spotted the man
across the dark room.

"Here is the woman,"
said the man.
"Meet Lupe Garcia."

Lupe and Benito
shook hands.
Benito liked
Lupe's looks.
She had
large, brown eyes.

Her long, dark hair
was pulled back.
She wore
a pretty Mexican dress.
She seemed too good
to be true.

Lupe liked
what she saw, too.
She liked
Benito's warm eyes
and kind face.

"I am so happy
that you speak Spanish,"
Benito told her.
He took her hand.

He passed
the 800 dollars
to the man.
The man
walked out the door.
Then Benito and Lupe
sat down
at a table.

"When did you
become an American?"
Benito asked Lupe.

"Well . . ."
Lupe began.
"I will tell you something.
But you must not tell
anyone else.
I bought a visa
to visit my aunt and uncle.
My uncle found me work
in a dress factory.
Then I got sick.
Then I changed
to a different dress factory.
I have stayed here
much too long.
I am not legal."

"What?"
cried Benito.
"That man
told me
you are American!
You and I

were supposed to get married.
Then I
could get my green card."

   "I am sorry,"
said Lupe.
"I do not even know
that man.
He is a friend
of someone I work with."

   "I just lost
a lot of money!"
cried Benito.
With that,
he stamped out
of the bar.
He was too angry
for words.

Thinking It Over

1. Why do you think
   Benito was willing
   to trust the stranger?

2. When you meet
   new people,
   how do you size them up?

CHAPTER 5

The man
was long gone.
Benito would never find him.
He had to face facts.
His 800 dollars were gone.

But Benito
could not stop thinking
about Lupe Garcia.
She was not American.
She could not help him
get a green card.
But Benito knew
he had to find her.
He had to see her again.

Night after night,
he went back
to the same place.
He looked for Lupe
in the crowd.

"Do you know
Lupe Garcia?"
he asked people there.
"She works
in a dress factory."

But nobody knew her.
Night after night,
he went home sad.

There was only one thing
left to do.
Benito would have to find
the place where she worked.
He rode the bus
all over Los Angeles.
Whenever he passed
a building that looked
like a dress factory,
Benito got off the bus.

He walked inside
each factory.
They all
were loud and hot.
"Is there a woman here

named Lupe Garcia?"
Benito asked.

"No—sorry,"
said someone
at each place.
But one day,
the answer
was not so clear.

"Is there a woman here
named Lupe Garcia?"
Benito asked.

"Who wants to know?"
the desk person wondered.

"Benito Cruz."

"Are you working
for the government?"

"Of course not,"
said Benito.
"Lupe Garcia
is a friend of mine."

"Lupe Garcia
does not work here,"
said the desk person.
"But she once did.
Maybe her friends
could help you out."

"Yes, I knew her,"
said one young woman.
"She lives
with her aunt and uncle
in East L.A."

"East L.A.
is a big place,"
said Benito.
"Do you know
which street?"

"On 6th Street,
I think,"
said the woman.
"Right near a park."

Benito
headed for East L.A.

The bus dropped him off
near the park.
He stopped
at every door.
He rang every bell.

"Do you know
a young woman
named Lupe Garcia?"
he asked everyone.

"No—sorry,"
was always the answer.

"I'll try
one more door,"
Benito said
to himself.
He rang twice.
A young woman
came down the stairs.
She opened the door.
She had long, dark hair.
Benito knew her eyes
right away.
It was Lupe.

Thinking It Over

1. How would you
   go about finding someone?

2. When do you know
   that something you want
   is worth a lot of trouble to get?

CHAPTER 6

Lupe was happy
to see Benito.
Benito told her
he was sorry
for what had happened.
Lupe understood.
She was just happy
Benito had tried so hard
to find her.

"Now I have found you,"
said Benito.
"What's next?
I've already lost 800 dollars
and a week of work.
I must get back
to the fields."

"Why don't you
stay in Los Angeles?"
Lupe asked.

"My uncle
can get you a job
in the lamp factory."

"Factory work—
I don't know,"
said Benito.
"I like to be outside.
But I would rather
be near you.
I will work
in the factory
for a little while."

Benito and Lupe
both worked long days.
Benito found
a place to live
down the street.
That way,
it was easy
to see each other
after work.

"I want
to marry you,"

Benito told Lupe
one night.

"I want
to marry you, too,"
said Lupe.
"But we cannot be married
in the U.S.
We are not legal."

"Let's go
to Mexico,"
said Benito.
"We can get married
in Mexico.
Then we can come back
to California."

"I am afraid
to cross the border again,"
said Lupe.
"Besides,
I want
my sister Raquel
to join me here.
I cannot go back.

I am afraid enough
that I will be caught
right here."

   "Then what
will we do?"
asked Benito.

   "We must go on
as we are,"
said Lupe.
"We can still
see each other.
I will keep on working
at the dress factory.
You will keep on working
at the lamp factory.
But we cannot get married.
And we must pay cash
for everything.
We cannot leave
a paper trail."

   "What is
a paper trail?"
Benito asked.

"Checks,
bank records,
things like that,"
said Lupe.
"All those papers
make a trail
that somebody could follow
to find us.
It could point out
that we are not legal.
I don't want
to be sent back
to Mexico
against my will."

"Is this
any way to live?"
asked Benito.

"There is
more for us here
than back home,"
said Lupe.
"You must remember
why we are here."

Thinking It Over

1. What would it be like
   to live
   in fear of being caught?

2. Would you live in a country
   without having papers?
   For what reasons?

3. Do you leave
   a "paper trail"?

CHAPTER 7

Every week
Lupe sent home
a money order.
She kept a record
of how much money
she had sent.
She hid the paper
in her room.
A few years
went by.
Lupe had sent enough
to help her family.
There was also enough
to bring Raquel
to Los Angeles.

"I have enough money,"
wrote Raquel.
"Now all I need
is a visa.

That could take time.
I must wait."

"Maybe Raquel
could buy a visa
the way I did,"
Lupe said to Benito.

"Don't you see?"
said Benito.
"A visa
should not cost money.
Your visa
was not real.
You were never legal
in this country.
Not even for one day."

"I know.
You are right,"
said Lupe.
"I want Raquel
to have real papers.
It is worth
the wait."

"Don't be silly,"
said Benito.
"She might never
get a visa.
She might never see
a better life.
She might die
as poor as she lived.
I think
we should go
and get her out!"

"I told you before,"
laughed Lupe.
"I do not want
to cross the border again."

"Do you want
your sister here
or not?"
Benito asked.
"If you do,
we must go and get her.
And while we
are in Mexico,
we can get married!"

"Yes, we could,"
said Lupe.
"We could kill two birds
with one stone.
I will think about
your idea."

Lupe told Aunt Juana
about Benito's idea.
"I think
you are crazy!"
said Aunt Juana.
"It would be nice
to bring Raquel here.
It would be nice
to get married.
But you might never
make it back here.
Why don't you wait?
Haven't you heard?
There might be a new law.
Under the new law
you could get
a green card!
Then you can get married
right here!"

"They will never pass
such a law!"
laughed Lupe.

A few days later,
she gave Benito
her answer.
"OK,"
she said.
"Let's try it.
Let's go to Mexico.
We will get married.
Then we will bring Raquel
back to Los Angeles."

Lupe did not tell
Aunt Juana or Uncle Ruben
where she was going.
She only said
she was going away.
A few days later
Lupe and Benito left.
They had no trouble
getting into Mexico.
That part of the trip
was easy.

Thinking It Over

1. Has anyone ever
   talked you into doing something
   you didn't want to do?

2. How do you
   talk someone into something?

3. What does it mean
   to "kill two birds with one stone"?

CHAPTER 8

Lupe and Benito
were on a bus
to Mexico City.
The bus stopped.
Lupe and Benito
got off.
They needed
something to eat.
They went
into a little place
along the road.
That is where
they heard the bad news.

"Mexico City
is a mess!"
Lupe heard a man say.
"Many, many people
lost their homes.
And many people
have been killed.

They don't know
how many yet.
They are still trying
to dig out the bodies!
Such bad luck!
The earthquake
hit the city itself!"

   "Did you hear that?"
Lupe asked Benito.
"An earthquake!
In Mexico City!
I hope
my family is all right!"

   "We'll just have to go
and find out!"
said Benito.

   They ate their food
in a hurry.
Then they caught
the next bus.

   What they found
in Mexico City

was very sad.
Many people's homes
were now in pieces.
Rock and wood
lay all over the place.
It was hard to tell
where some streets had been.
Children cried
for their mothers.
Mothers called
their children's names.
Red Cross workers
dug into the mess
to follow the cries.

Lupe and Benito
got close
to Lupe's old home.
Lupe saw some people
she knew.
"Have you seen
anyone from my family?"
she asked them.
They shook their heads.
She asked everyone
in sight.

She was afraid
to hear an answer.

At last,
someone had an answer.
"Your whole family
was lost,"
said an old woman.
"I am sorry.
They are all dead.
I saw some men
carry them away
this morning."

"Raquel, too?"
asked Lupe.

"I'm afraid so,"
said the old woman.

"Oh, Benito!"
cried Lupe.
"Why was I
not here?
Why am I
not dead, too?"

"Because you
were in luck,"
said Benito.
"You and I—
we are safe.
We can go back
to Los Angeles.
Your sister Raquel
never got to try."

Lupe did not feel safe.
But she
took care of matters
in Mexico City.
She found out
that her family
had been buried
with many other people
in a huge grave.
She said goodbye
to what had been her home.
There was no one and nothing
left for her here.
It was time
to head north again.

Thinking It Over

1. When do you know
it is time to leave a place?

2. Have you ever felt
like the lucky one?

CHAPTER 9

"Why don't we
get married
before we leave?"
asked Benito.

"I love you,"
said Lupe.
"But this is not
a good time.
I am so sad
about my family.
I want to be happy
on my wedding day.
And Mexico City
is in such bad shape.
I just want
to go to Los Angeles."

"Maybe you are right,"
said Benito.

"But when
will we ever get married?"

  "There will be
a right time,"
said Lupe.
"Please—
let's leave Mexico now."

  "Off we go!"
said Benito.
"You will see
how easy it is
to cross the border.
You will see
that we can come and go
as we please.
We can come back
another time
to get married."

  Lupe and Benito
headed for California.
They walked
along the road
until they got a ride.

When they got close
to the border,
the driver
dropped them off.
Benito and Lupe
sat down.
They waited
until it got dark.
Then they saw a big truck.

   "Here is our ride
across the border!"
said Benito.
He waved his arm
in the air.
The truck stopped.
Benito handed money
to the driver.

   "Get in the back!"
said the driver.

   Benito and Lupe
walked to the back
of the truck.
Benito knocked

on the back door.
Someone inside
opened the door.
Benito and Lupe
climbed in.

"See how easy?"
laughed Benito.

The truck
was hot and dark.
Lupe could not see faces.
But she could hear
the sounds of many people.
Some had bad colds.
Some made loud noises
in their sleep.
A bad smell
hung in the heavy air.

"How soon
will we get out of here?"
she asked Benito.

"Not long,"
he answered.

In a little while,
the truck stopped.
Benito and Lupe
heard someone
banging on the truck.
All of a sudden
the back door opened.
A man stood there.
Lupe and Benito
knew right away
who he was.
He worked
for the U.S. border patrol.

"Everyone out!"
shouted the man.

One by one,
40 people
jumped off the truck.

"Stand over here!"
the man called out.
"Everyone wait here.
I will be back
in ten minutes."

The group waited.
No one ran away.

"Where are we?"
Lupe asked.

Benito looked around.
"We're in California."

"You mean
we got caught
when we crossed the border?"
asked Lupe.

"It looks that way,"
said Benito.

"I'm afraid,"
said Lupe.

"Why be afraid?"
said Benito.
"This is just
our hard-luck life.
Let's wait
and see what happens."

Thinking It Over

1. Why do you think
   only one man
   stopped the truck?

2. If you were in the group,
   would you have waited
   for the man to come back?

3. What do you think
   will happen to Benito and Lupe?

CHAPTER 10

The border guard
came back
in a bus.
All the Mexicans
had waited for him.

"Everyone get on the bus!"
he called out.

All the Mexicans
got on the bus.
The little bus
was crowded.
There were not enough seats
for everyone.

The bus
turned around
in the road.
It was headed
back to Mexico.

Lupe saw
a little marker
on the road.
That must mean
we crossed the border,
she said to herself.
The land
looked the same
on both sides
of the marker.
All she could see
was sand and brush
all around.
About a mile
past the marker,
the bus stopped.

"Now everyone out!"
called the man.
"Go home!
And don't come back!
If you try,
I'll just take you back again!"

The bus
pulled away.

The group waited
until the bus
was out of sight.
Then some of them
began to walk
toward California.

"Let's go!"
said Benito to Lupe.
"We are only
a mile from the border!"

"We might as well,"
said Lupe.
"To me,
the land
looks all the same.
Why is this sand Mexico
and that sand California?"

"I don't know,"
said Benito.
"Why were we born
in poor Mexico?
Why must we
go to such trouble

to make a living?
Why can't we
get married
in the United States?
There are
too many things
to ask *why* about.
Things are
as they are.
We do what we must."

And by the moon's light,
they crossed the line again.

Thinking It Over

1. Would you try again
   to cross the border?

2. What things
   do you ask "why" about?

3. When have you had to
   "do what you must"?

CHAPTER 11

Back in Los Angeles,
Benito was not happy.
He did not like
city life.

"All the vegetables
are in season now,"
he said.
"I must go.
I must find
some farm work."

Lupe begged him
not to leave.
She told him
about the law
that might be passed.
"Just think!"
she said.
"We could get
our green cards.

We could get married
right here!
And then we can find
better jobs!"

"Who knows
if the law
will ever come about?"
said Benito.
"It might never happen.
I cannot wait.
I must leave.
I will see you
as often as I can."

Benito and Lupe
held on to each other.

"Say we'll be together
sometime soon,"
cried Lupe.

"I hope so,"
said Benito.
And he was off
for the fields.

At his first job
the field workers
were treated badly.
They had to live
in tiny huts
that were no better than
holes in the ground.
Benito took a job
at another farm
as soon as he could.
All summer,
he picked
fresh vegetables.

That fall,
the new law passed.
Not everyone
liked the law.
But for people
like Lupe Garcia,
it was good news.
She had lived
in the U.S.
since before 1982.
All she had to do
was show that fact.

Then she could be legal.
In another 18 months,
she could get
a green card!

The law
could help Benito, too.
He had lived
in both the U.S. and Mexico.
But Benito
had done farm work
in the U.S.
for 90 days
during the past year.

Even so,
Lupe did not know
where Benito was now.
She wondered
if he had heard
about the law.
She did not know
how to reach him.
All she could do
was wait
to hear from him.

Thinking It Over

1. Do you think
   Lupe and Benito
   should be able
   to get green cards?

2. Would you rather work
   in a factory or a field?

3. Do you think
   Benito will come back?

CHAPTER **12**

"I'm going ahead
without Benito,"
Lupe told Aunt Juana.
"I will try
to get my green card."

"Can you show
you have been here
since before 1982?"
asked Aunt Juana.
"You were
always so careful
not to leave
a paper trail."

"This is true,"
said Lupe.
"I have
no paper trail.
But you will see!"

   An office
was set up
to help people
become legal.
The office
was small.
Not enough people
worked there.
There was not enough room
to store everyone's papers.
But Lupe
went to the office.
It was her only hope.

   People in line
held piles of papers.
They wanted to show
they had lived
in the U.S.
long enough.
Lupe held
just one piece of paper.

   At last,
it was Lupe's turn.

"This is all you have?"
asked the woman.
"Just one paper?
What is it?"

Lupe pulled out
the paper.
It was the record
of all the money orders
she had sent
to Raquel.
There was a date
next to each one.
The record began
on August 9, 1980.

"This is the best
I can do,"
said Lupe.
"I hope
it is enough."

"It is not much,"
said the woman.
"But it does go back
to before 1982.

We will let you know
if it is OK."

   Now Lupe
had two things
to wait for—
Benito and the U.S. government.
She was afraid.
She could get
one, both, or none
of her wishes.
With all her heart,
she wanted both.

   One morning,
the doorbell rang.
Lupe ran down
to answer it.

   "You have some mail!"
said Benito Cruz.

   Lupe threw her arms
around Benito.
"You're here!"
she cried.

"And so is
your letter
from the government!"
said Benito.

Lupe tore open
the mail.
Inside was the word
she had been waiting for.
The money order record
had won Lupe
her magic paper!

"And now
you are next!"
she said to Benito.
"Can you show
you worked on a farm?"

Benito pulled a paper
out of his pocket.
It was a note
from the farm company
he worked for.
"This should do it!"
he cried.

"We can get married
as soon as I get
my magic paper!"

"This paper
is worth its weight in gold!"
cried Lupe.

"It is worth
more than gold!"
said Benito.
"It is worth everything
in the world
to you and me!"

"Of course!"
cried Lupe.
She held Benito
with all her might.
For the first time
in seven years,
she felt safe.

Thinking It Over

1. What makes you feel safe?

2. Why can a piece of paper be so important?

3. Do you feel that anything is magic?